# The Pied Piper of Hamelin

## A GERMAN FOLKTALE

retold by Amanda StJohn • illustrated by Dianna Bonder

Distributed by The Child's World®
1980 Lookout Drive • Mankato, MN 56003-1705
800-599-READ • www.childsworld.com

Acknowledgments
The Child's World®: Mary Berendes, Publishing Director
The Design Lab: Kathleen Petelinsek, Design
Red Line Editorial: Editorial direction

Library of Congress Cataloging-in-Publication Data
StJohn, Amanda, 1982–
   The Pied Piper of Hamelin : a German folktale / by Amanda StJohn ;
illustrated by Dianna Bonder.
       p. cm.
   Summary: The town of Hamelin is overrun with rats, but when the Pied
Piper who gets rid of them is refused payment he takes the children away
from their greedy parents.
   ISBN 978-1-60973-142-7 (library reinforced : alk. paper)
   [1. Folklore–Germany.] I. Bonder, Dianna, 1970– ill. II. Pied Piper of
Hamelin. English. III. Title.
   PZ8.1.S8577Pie 2012
   398.20943'02—dc23                                    2011010923

Printed in the United States of America in Mankato, Minnesota.
July 2011
PA02086

h, do not be afraid of my pet rats, Bernhard and Käse! They do not bite! They wish to hear a story, just as you do.

Do you know the German word for rats? It is *ratten!* The people of Hamelin town in Germany know this word very well. You see, once Hamelin had a problem. Rats were everywhere! And the people wanted to get rid of all the rats in town. . . .

Imagine a house, just one house, filled
with furry rats. Rats are on the ceiling,
on the stairs, and on the dinner table.
A frightened woman stands on a chair.
She screams and swings her soup ladle to
keep rats out of her hair.

In Hamelin town, every house looked
exactly this way! Every shop, even the
candy store, was filled with greedy rats
with sharp teeth. They ate everything
in sight.

"*Ratten, ratten!*" cried the butcher.
"The rats have eaten all my hams!"

"*Ratten!*" shrieked a mother. "They
are carrying away my Sam!"

6

The carpenter built large rattraps,
but the rats were too smart to be caught.
They snapped the traps shut with a whip
of the tail and gobbled all the cheese.
Then, before the milkmaid blinked, they
slipped into her milk pails and washed
the cheese down with a drink.

The people were running out of food.
Their houses were beginning to crumble.
Their hats had all been chewed!

The blacksmith decided what the people should do next. "Let's ask the mayor. He will know what is best!"

"Mayor," huffed the blacksmith, "we've all been quite patient, but now something must be done, no matter what it costs! Find a way to rid Hamelin of rats, or we'll boot you right out of town."

"I don't know a thing about getting rid of pests!" moaned the mayor once the people left. "I wish I had some help!"

Can you believe it? The moment the mayor wished for help—*tap-tap-tappity-tap*. Someone was knocking on his front door. Do you know who was on the other side?

The mayor opened the door to reveal a stranger from a distant land. His eyes were as blue as gumballs. His hair was long and white. His robe was pied—half yellow and half red. Around his neck hung a golden pipe.

"I am the Pied Piper," the man proclaimed. "With this pipe, I'll play an enchanting tune to draw Hamelin's rats away. There's just one thing. . . . I don't work for free. One thousand gold pieces is my usual fee."

The mayor excused himself to have a moment to think. He ran into a closet that closed with a squeak.

"There is enough gold in the treasury to pay the piper, but it would be nice to keep some of it for myself," the mayor whispered to himself.

From the closet the greedy mayor appeared. He gave a firm nod to the piper. "Let's do it, then. When the last rat is gone, I'll see to it that you are paid."

The Pied Piper stepped into the street and gave his pipe a blow. It peeped and pipped and bleeped and blipped, and the rats danced toward it.

Wherever the Pied Piper walked, the rats danced right behind him. He waltzed them to the edge of town where the Weser River waited.

Then, with a fancy trill, the pipe sang loud and clear. It caused the rats to jump into the river, and they drowned.

"Piper! Piper!" the townspeople cheered. "He came and played his little pipe, and the *ratten* disappeared!"

"Good people," the piper responded. "Thank you for praising my work. But you can thank me best by paying me what it is worth—a thousand gold pieces is what your mayor promised me. Now that you have your town back, this price should seem small."

"A thousand gold pieces?!" the blacksmith balked. "You must be joking! You hardly played one song. You only danced about!"

"Yeah!" the people shouted with meanness in their eyes. "You only danced about!"

Then the mayor came forward. "I promised you'd be paid, and I stick to my word. Here's one gold coin. Now get on your way!"

"*Ratten . . . ratten . . .*" the Pied Piper chided, pointing at the crowd. "I can see what kind of people you are now. Since you will not pay me, I shall play another song for you on my way out of town."

"Go ahead, Mr. Piper," shouted the baker's wife. "Play any tune you like! We know that all the rats are dead. They won't be coming back."

Without a twitch of anger, the piper lifted the pipe to his lips. It tweetled and deedled and toodled, until something in the town rumbled.

*BaaaaaROOOM!* From every corner of every house, children came running to the piper. They giggled and laughed, skipped and bounced. Some ran right out of their diapers!

The piper waltzed them to a mountainside. Then, with a *whistle, whistle, woooo*, the mountain opened like a secret door. It welcomed the children and piper to come inside.

That was the last that Hamelin saw of its children, and the Pied Piper, too.

With all the rats and children gone,
the people of Hamelin had no one to
blame for the destruction of their town
except themselves. They all decided to
change their greedy ways. And, when
they promised to pay a person for
services, they kindly kept their word.

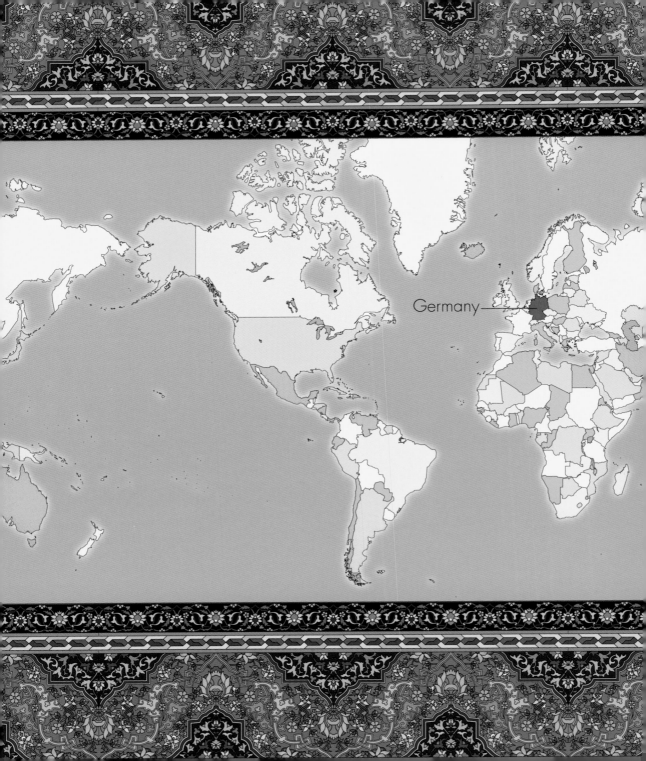

Germany

# FOLKTALES

**F**olktales are adventurous, magical stories. In *The Pied Piper*, finding out how the people of Hamelin solve their rat problem is quite an adventure. The mysterious Pied Piper and his magic pipe play a large part in it.

Folktales have heroes and villains. In *The Pied Piper*, it is difficult to tell whether the characters are good guys or bad guys. At first, we feel bad for the townspeople, who have a terrible problem and need help to solve it. Later, we discover that the people can be mean and greedy. *The Pied Piper* teaches us to be honest and fair. Folktales are written to teach us lessons, just like this.

*The Pied Piper* takes place in a city that really exists. Hamelin, Germany can be found on a map. You can also find the Weser River and Poppenberg Mountain.

Folktale means "a story that the people tell." A historical document says that a rat-catcher really did visit Hameln during the Middle Ages. He rid the city of rats, and later took the children away when parents refused to pay the piper's fee. So, what did the people do to remember this event? They told the story, over and over, to anyone who would listen. Eventually, a storyteller wrote the story down for folks, and thus the folktale of *The Pied Piper* has been kept alive for hundreds of years.

# ABOUT THE ILLUSTRATOR

**D**ianna Bonder has been illustrating children's books for the past 12 years. Dianna lives in her very own faraway fairy-tale place, called Gabriola Island just off the coast of British Columbia, Canada. Her days are filled with laughter and art with her two daughters, two cats, and two dogs.

24